The Man Who Knew Too Much

Clarion Books
a Houghton Mifflin Company imprint
215 Park Avenue South, New York, NY 10003
Text copyright © 1994 by Julius Lester
Illustrations copyright © 1994 by Leonard Jenkins

The illustrations for this book were executed in oil paint on cardboard.
The text was set in 15/20 pt. Ehrhardt.

For information about permission to reproduce selections from this
book, write to Permissions, Houghton Mifflin Company, 215 Park
Avenue South, New York, NY 10003.

Printed in the USA

Library of Congress Cataloging-in-Publication Data

Lester, Julius.
    The man who knew too much : a moral tale from the Baila of
Zambia / by Julius Lester ; illustrated by Leonard Jenkins.
        p.   cm.
    Summary: A husband does not believe it when his wife tells
him that their crying baby is comforted by a huge eagle who flies down
with its sharp talons and alights on the baby.
    ISBN 0-395-60521-0
    [1. Folklore, Ila. 2. Folklore—Zambia.] I. Jenkins, Leonard,
ill. II. Title.
            PZ8.1.L434Man   1994   93-40810
            398.24'5/8916—dc20   CIP
            [E]   AC

HOR 10 9 8 7 6 5 4 3 2 1

The Man Who Knew Too Much

A Moral Tale from the Baila of Zambia

Retold by JULIUS LESTER

Illustrated by Leonard Jenkins

CLARION BOOKS/ New York

A woman had a child.
The simple events are not simple.
The rising and setting of the sun.
The wind.
The rain.
The beating of our hearts and the breath
in our bodies.

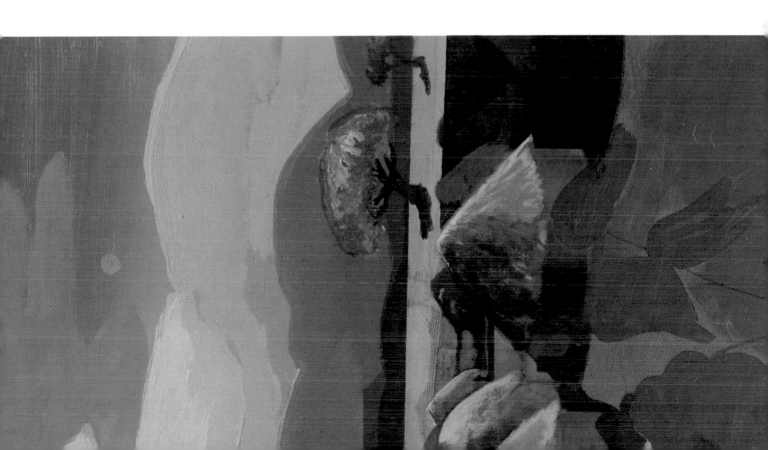

A woman had a child.
A woman carried life within her and, at
the appointed time, it came forth.
Creation was renewed.

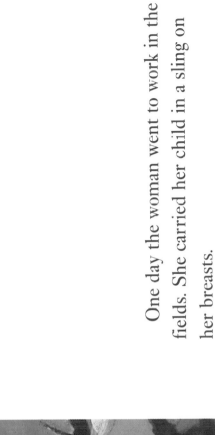

One day the woman went to work in the fields. She carried her child in a sling on her breasts.

As she began hoeing, the child awoke and started crying.

The woman stopped her work, sat down in the shade of a nearby tree, and nursed the child. When the child was asleep, the woman laid it in the shade and returned to her work.

No sooner had she done so than the child awoke, crying.

The woman was annoyed. She had much work to do. How was she to get it done if the child wouldn't sleep?

She sighed, put down her hoe, and started toward the child.

Suddenly, out of the sky came a large eagle. The flapping of its wings was like the sound of thunder and the woman watched as the eagle came closer and closer toward her child. The eagle pulled up its great wings and landed on the baby.

The eagles of this land were mighty birds. They were so strong that they easily killed and ate monkeys, jackals, and small antelope.

The mother saw the bird with its sharp talons sitting on her child, its wings moving slowly like storm clouds gathering during rainy season.

The baby was quiet now. The woman feared the eagle had torn out her child's heart. She grabbed the hoe and ran toward the eagle, her heart pounding like the feet of elephants in stampede. The eagle turned its head, saw her, and spreading its wings, flew away.

Terrified, the mother looked at her child. It slept peacefully. She looked for the blood that the eagle's talons must have made.

There was no blood. There was not even a scratch.

She stood slowly and stared at the sky into which the eagle had vanished. She didn't know what to think. Had she frightened the eagle away before it could kill her baby? She had seen the eagle sitting on her baby. Its talons should have left deep scratches and cuts. But there were none, and her baby slept peacefully where before it had been crying.

"It's a marvel!" she whispered.

For the rest of the day, the baby slept and the woman got much work done.

That evening she returned to the village and her home. She wanted to tell her husband of the marvel she had witnessed. But she said nothing. How could she tell her husband that an eagle had comforted their child?

Too, she needed time to be alone with the wonder of what she had seen. Sometimes, we must guard what is inside us, refusing to share it with anyone. There are matters which belong to us alone. It is as much love not to share.

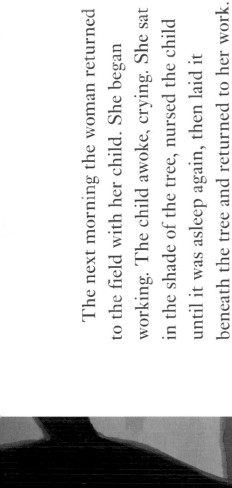

The next morning the woman returned to the field with her child. She began working. The child awoke, crying. She sat in the shade of the tree, nursed the child until it was asleep again, then laid it beneath the tree and returned to her work.

No sooner had she done so than the child awoke, crying. This time the woman waited.

And yes, the eagle came out of the sky and landed on the child. It moved its wings up and down slowly, comforting the child until it was once more quiet and then asleep.

The woman watched, knowing the eagle would not harm her child and yet, afraid. When she could stand it no longer, she picked up her hoe and ran to the child. The eagle turned its head, saw her, and spreading its wings, flew into the sky.

The woman examined her child. As before, the child was unharmed and slept peacefully.

"What a wondrous thing!" the woman exclaimed. "I must tell my husband!" She picked up the baby and ran to the village.

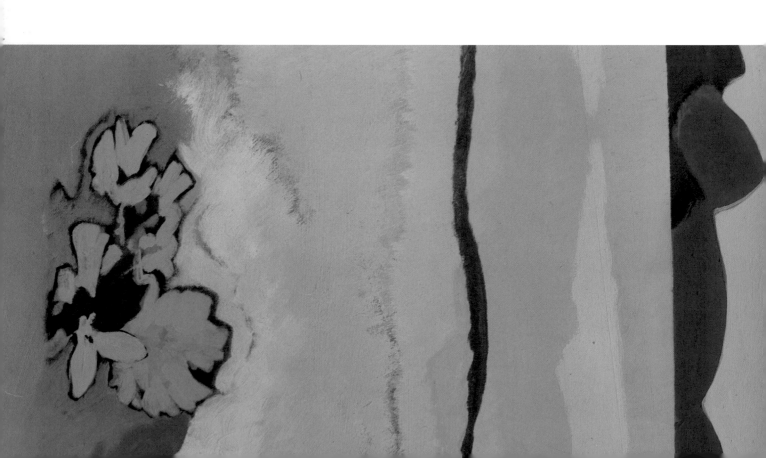

When she told her husband what had happened, he said, "You've been standing in the sun too long. I've seen eagles kill antelope big enough to feed us for a week. I believe you must've lost your mind!"

The woman was hurt that her husband did not believe her. Because she was hurt, she became angry. "Come to the field with me and see for yourself. We'll see who's crazy!"

Sometimes we are privileged to witness and experience great wonders, and it is natural to want to share them with those we love. But if they reject what we say, we should be silent. A wonder can never be proved. It is there, alive as the fire in the sun, for those who *know* what they *don't know*.

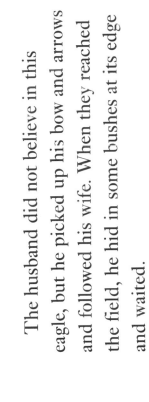

The husband did not believe in this eagle, but he picked up his bow and arrows and followed his wife. When they reached the field, he hid in some bushes at its edge and waited.

The child, awake and crying, was laid beneath the tree by its mother. She went to the field and picked up her hoe, and waited.

The eagle came out of the sky.

The father saw in horror. He had seen the spear-like talons of eagles rip flesh from jackals. He remembered how their beaks, like knives, tore the throats of antelopes, causing the blood to gush forth hot like sand.

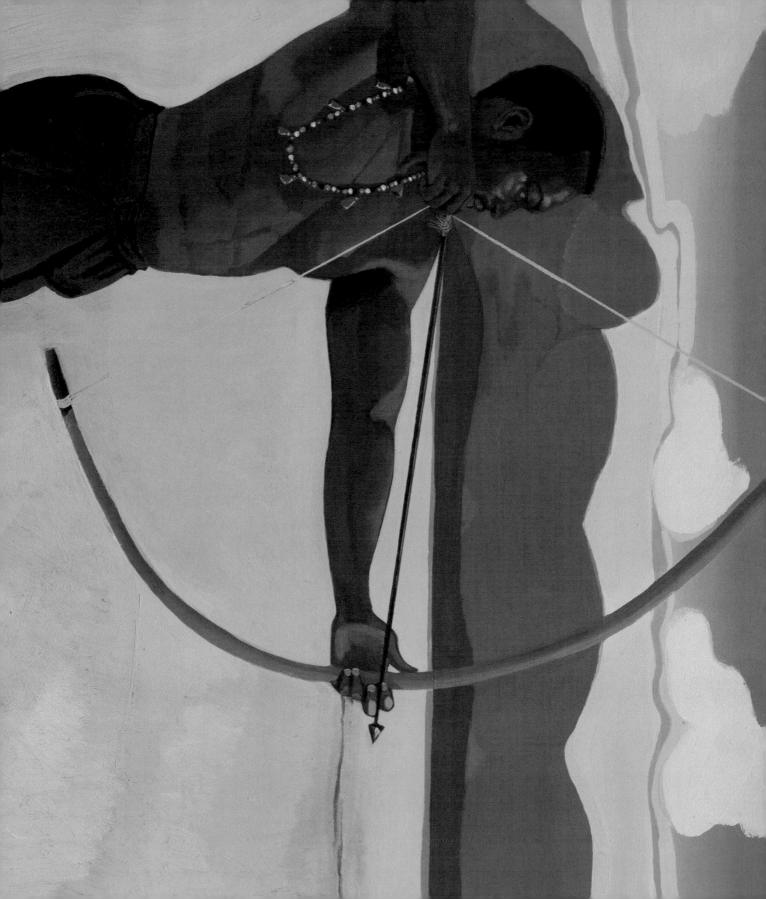

Seeing the eagle sitting on their child, he strung his bow with an arrow, and pulling the bow with all his strength, he let the arrow go.

As he watched the swift, silent flight of the arrow, he saw the eagle fly up at the last instant. The arrow sank with a soft sound into the body of his baby, killing it.

The eagle flew at the man and cursed him, saying, "Now is kindness among people at an end because you have killed your child. Beginning now and forevermore, people shall kill one another."

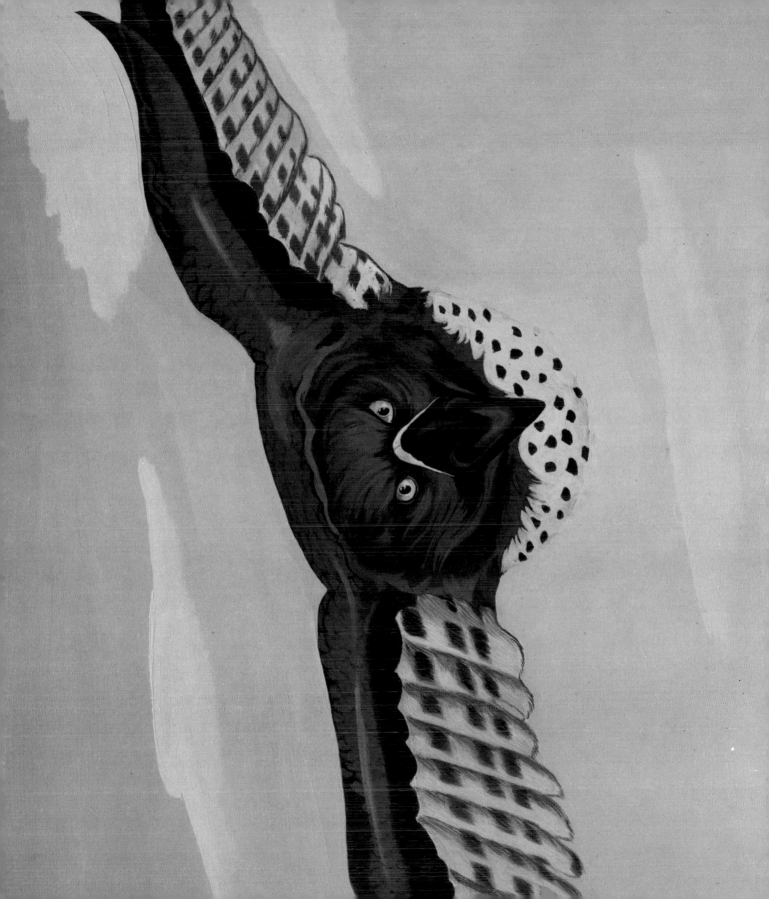

And that is how murder came into the world. The man knew too much, because he thought he *knew* what he had never seen and never experienced.

Notes on the Story

One day in the mid-seventies, I went with a friend to watch a puppet show performance in Central Park in New York City. One of the tales the puppeteers performed was an African story called "The Child and the Eagle." I was deeply moved by the story and was told that it could be found in Paul Radin's *African Folktales* (Princeton, Bollingen Series, 1970).

In the late seventies, I reworked the tale, and since then, have told it many times. Each retelling has been a reworking until it has acquired this form—for now.

Reworking the tale in this instance means several things. The original tale is spare in language and detail. I have added fictional elements—the descriptions of the eagle, the details, the heightening of tension, etc. Additionally, I have added the voice of a storyteller who interprets at critical points in the story, making explicit the meaning behind the events. Finally, I have replaced the sparse language of the original with a language richer in metaphor and simile, a language that is simultaneously formal and poetic.

This remarkable tale is from the Baila people of Zambia. While some may think the story too "gruesome" for children, it is less so than the average Saturday morning cartoon, and no more so than many European folktales. The difference is that in cartoons and European tales, it is the "villain" who reaches a bad end. Here, it is the child.

The story provides an opportunity for adults to consider those times when a child has felt "killed" when an adult did something that took away the child's sense of wonder and marvel in an experience. The tale provides an opportunity to talk about the importance of keeping some experiences secret; to talk about the "marvels" in everyday life; to talk about how important it is to know what you know and know what you don't know.

The object of the tale is not to horrify, but to teach us how to decrease the number of occasions we kill wonder and awe and the marvel that living could be—if we could only be still and allow it.